UNEARTH
VOL 2

UNEARTH

When unexplained mass mutations ravage a remote village in Mexico, a scientific task force travels to the inhospitable area to investigate the contamination. Tracing the source of the phenomenon to a nearby cave system, the team discovers a bizarre, hostile ecosystem and a supernatural revelation from which they may never escape.

THE STORY SO FAR:

Dr. Amelia Reyes and Dr. Frankie McCommick, beset upon from all sides by murderous, unknown biology, must fight to keep their sanity as their team members begin to change in otherworldly fashion.

Amidst a bloodbath, the truth of the mass mutations is revealed: A slumbering ancient Being is transforming humans into its own anatomy to heal itself from an eons-old injury.

Partially regenerated, the Being awakens and erupts from the Earth.

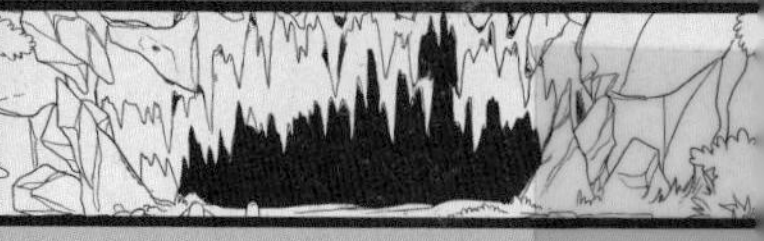

AMELIA

Dr. Reyes was the leader of the scientific task force during the initial investigation of Site 17 and was Dr. Frankie McCommick's best friend. Haunted by the disappearance of her daughter years before, she succumbed to madness. Amelia was was killed by Frankie in self-defense.

ISAAC

A little boy living on Henry Thomas's commune. Since his parents left he longs for a family.

HENRY

Henry Thomas is a charismatic leader. In the new world he has gathered together wayward believers to live together in peace.

CAST OF CHARACTERS & KEY PERSONNEL

FRANKIE
Dr. McCommick was part of the initial investigation team looking into the strange occurrences in Mexico. Her darkest moment was killing her best friend, Amelia, in self-defense.

KING
King was a member of the military task force investigating Site 17. A selfless leader, he bought time for Frankie and Nails to escape with their lives.

NAILS
Private First Class Catherine Nunez is as tough as her nickname, and is one of the only survivors of the incident in Mexico.

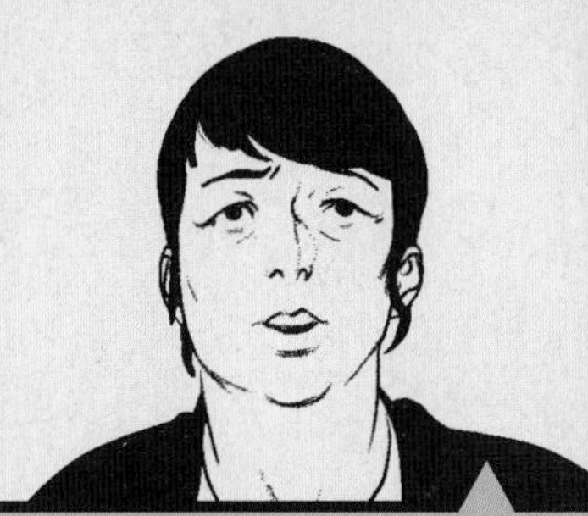

FERNIE
The estranged ex-wife of Major Kul. The two haven't spoken in years.

KUL
An army Major who has been involved in this mess since the beginning. In a futile effort to contain the erruption at Site 17, he bombed the surrounding villages and killed thousands.

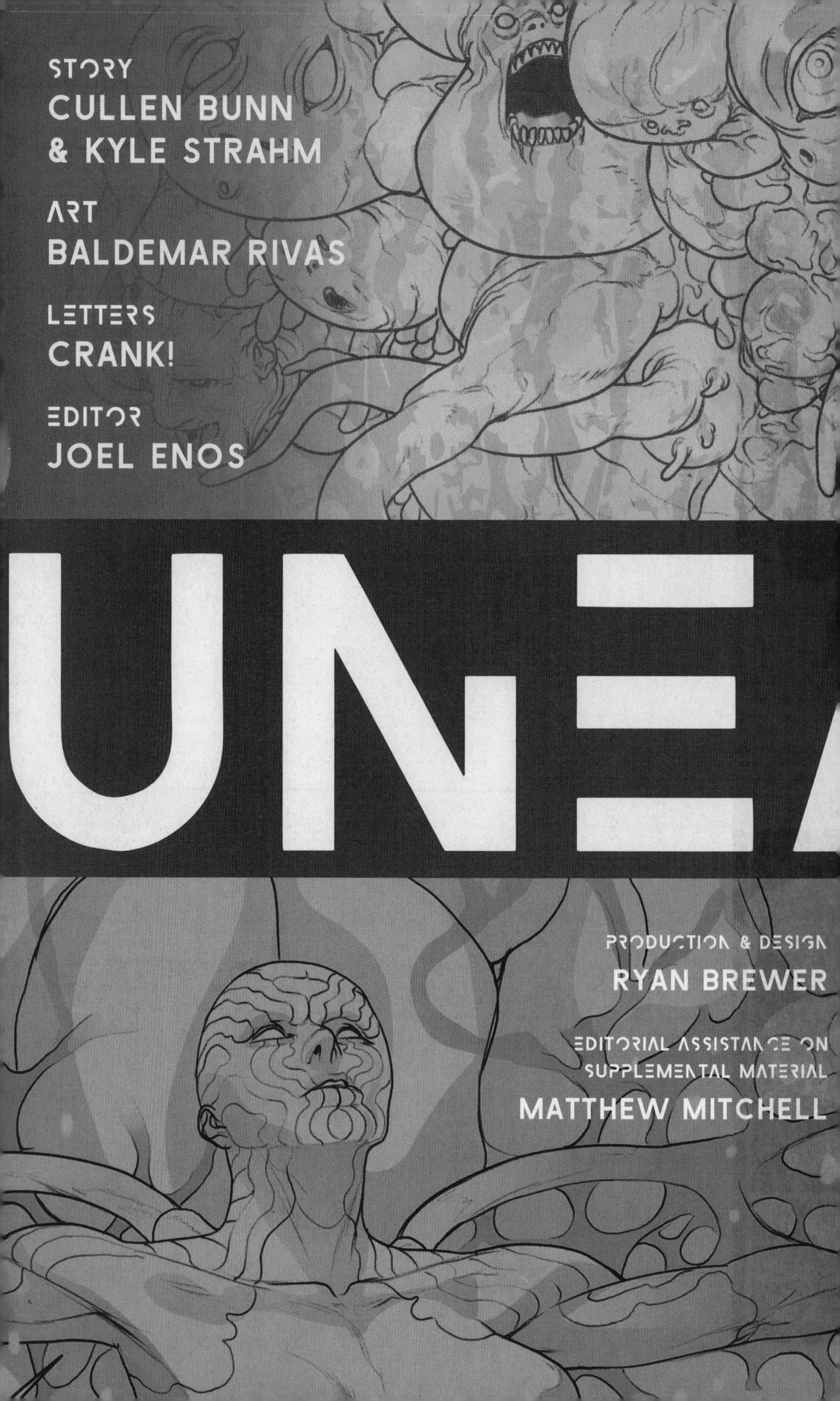

STORY
CULLEN BUNN
& KYLE STRAHM

ART
BALDEMAR RIVAS

LETTERS
CRANK!

EDITOR
JOEL ENOS

UNEA

PRODUCTION & DESIGN
RYAN BREWER

EDITORIAL ASSISTANCE ON
SUPPLEMENTAL MATERIAL
MATTHEW MITCHELL

BONUS STORIES

"UNSETTLED"

STORY
KING EDDIE

ART
MARCO DEFILLO

"EL CAZADOR"

STORY
MATTHEW MITCHELL

ART
KRISTOFOR HARRIS

UNEARTH, VOL. 2. First printing. May 2021. Published by Image Comics, Inc. Office of publication: PO BOX 14457, Portland, OR 97293. ISBN: 978-1-5343-1693-5.

Ch 06

NOW.

ONE YEAR AFTER MANIFESTATION.

WHEN MOST PEOPLE SEE THE **BLACKOUT ZONE** FOR THE FIRST TIME, THEY **HURL**.

I SEEN A LOT OF SHIT, BUT THIS TWENTY SQUARE MILES HAS SOMETHIN' EXTRA THAT GROSSES OUT YER **DNA**.

SO, HOW'S DAY ONE, **NAILS?**

DID YOU **FLASH THE HASH** YET?

NO, SIR, **LIEUTENANT MESNER!**

I HAVEN'T PUKED ALL YEAR.

IT'S ABOUT TIME YOU A-HOLES SHOWED UP!
WE'VE BEEN SENDIN' UP FLARES FOR A WEEK!
GRRRRRRRAWL

GODDAMN, I'M SO GLAD YOU'RE HERE.
WE'D HAVE LEFT DURIN' THE EVAC, BUT MY PHONE STOPPED WORKIN'.
I COULDN'T GET MY MAP NO MORE.
THE BILL WAS PAID, TOO. PHONE JUST STOPPED.

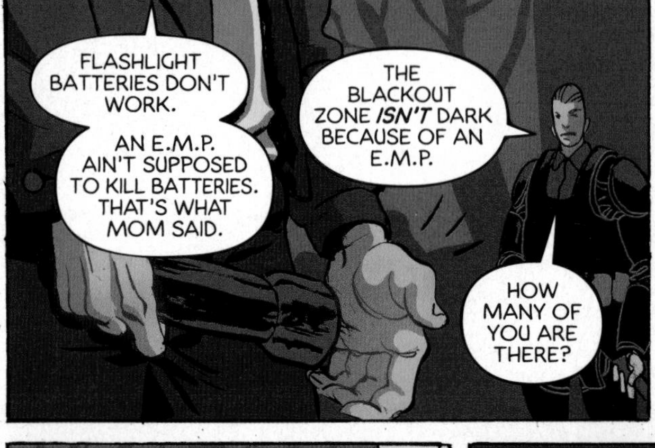
FLASHLIGHT BATTERIES DON'T WORK.
AN E.M.P. AIN'T SUPPOSED TO KILL BATTERIES. THAT'S WHAT MOM SAID.
THE BLACKOUT ZONE ISN'T DARK BECAUSE OF AN E.M.P.
HOW MANY OF YOU ARE THERE?

JUST THE THREE OF US, AND LUNDY THERE.
OH...

...AND MOM. SHE'S IN THE HOUSE.

SHE'S GONE THROUGH SOME CHANGES.

YOU'RE UP, NAILS. SHOW US WHAT YOU GOT.

YESSIR.

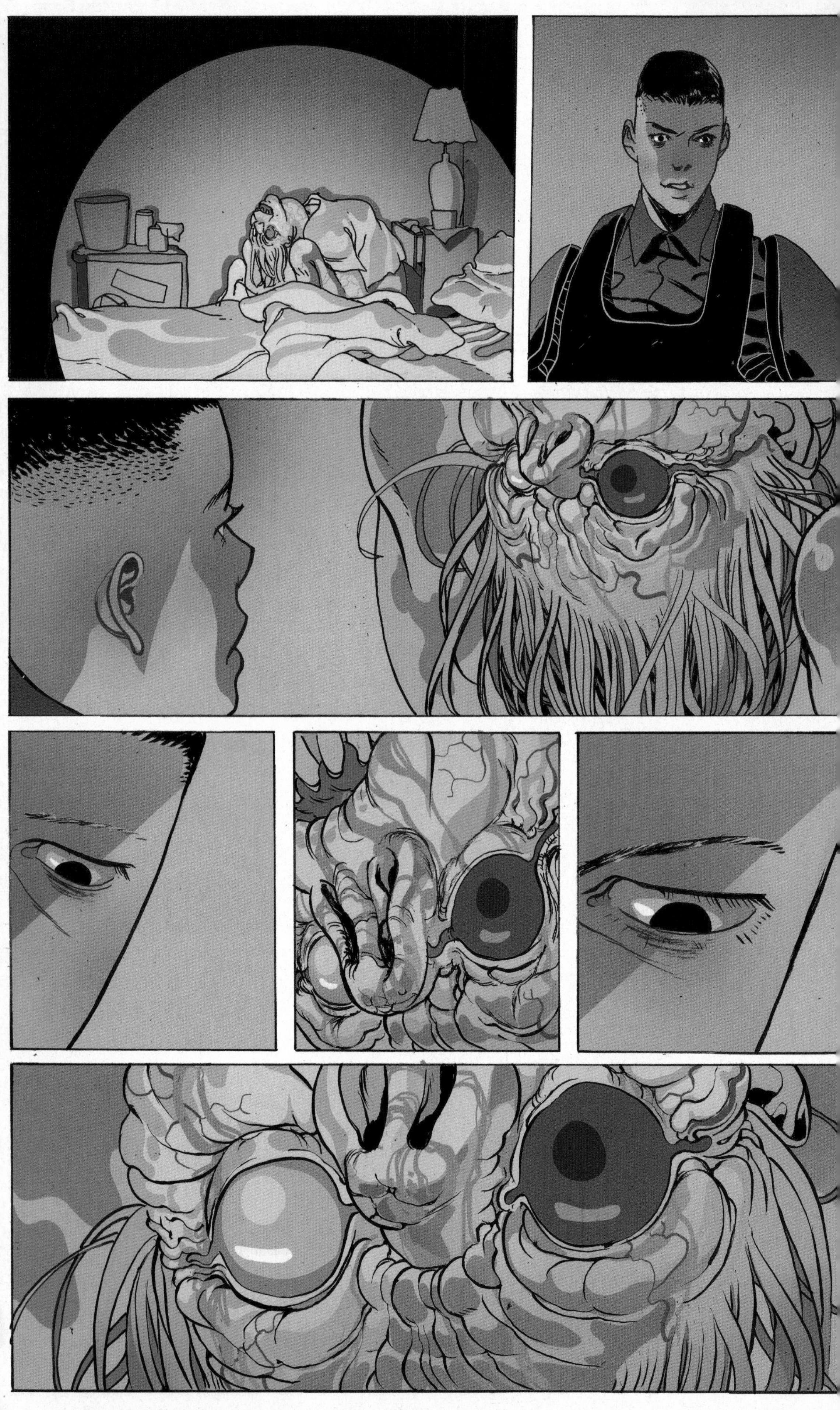

POP
POP

CAN'T *HESITATE* WITH THESE SUMBITCHES, PRIVATE.
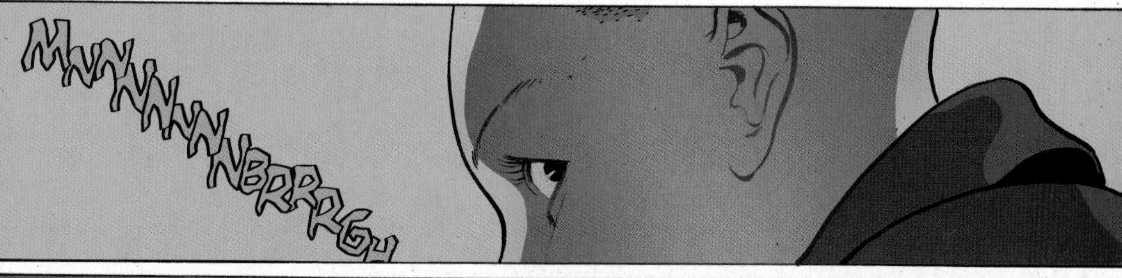
MNNNNNNNBRRRRGH

HHHSSSSSSSSSSS

NNGGG--
CHRIST!

SKRTCH
SKRTCH
SKRK

YOU ALL RIGHT, NAILS?
I THINK SO.
CLAWS DIDN'T CUT THROUGH THE VEST.
THAT THING... LOOKED DIFFERENT... ACTED DIFFERENT.
I'VE NEVER SEEN THEM MOVE THAT--
BRAKKA BRAKKA
SHOOT IT!
SHOOT IT!
MOMMA! NO!
AHHHHHRRRG!
BLAHG

SIR?
WHAT IS IT, PRIVATE?
THE SEARCH TEAM--THEY'VE RETURNED.
THEY'VE ENCOUNTERED SOMETHING.
SOMETHING *NEW*.

OL' NAILS CAME BACK?
THE THING THEY FOUND... THEY SAID IT WAS AGGRESSIVE.
IF THOSE MUTANTS ARE ORGANS, THIS THING IS LIKE A CLAW.

I WANT A FULL DEBRIEF.
BUT... NOT HERE.
WE'LL DO IT IN ONE OF THE OTHER UNITS.

IT'S TOO DAMN *CROWDED* IN HERE AS IT IS.

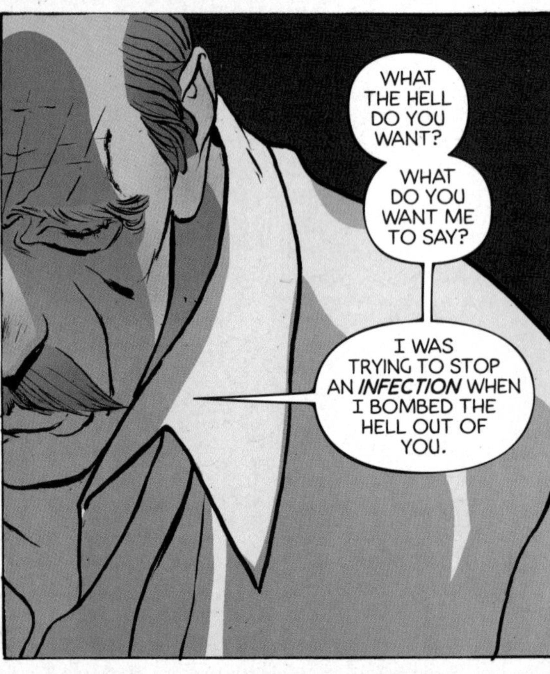
WHAT THE HELL DO YOU WANT?
WHAT DO YOU WANT ME TO SAY?
I WAS TRYING TO STOP AN *INFECTION* WHEN I BOMBED THE HELL OUT OF YOU.

AIN'T MY FAULT IT DIDN'T WORK.
AIN'T MY FAULT...

...YOU WERE *EXPENDABLE*.

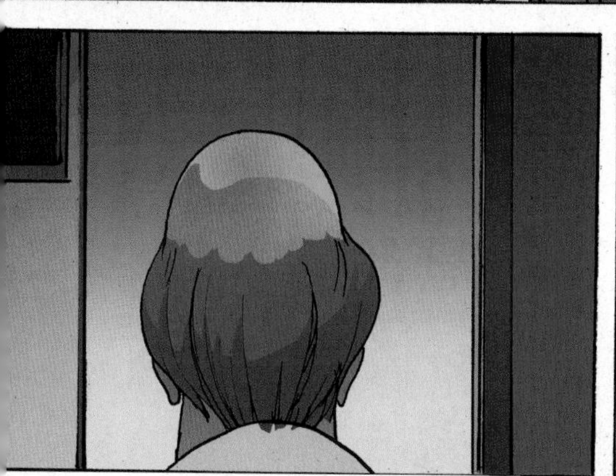

BATTERY'S *DEAD.*
GOT BETTER THINGS TO DO THAN CHARGE MY DAMN SMOKES.
GUESS I CAN'T BLAME *YOU* FOR THIS ONE, *HUH?*

I SHOULDN'T...

...BUT I'M GOING TO ANYWAY.

SIX MONTHS AGO.
"THE SKY IS DIFFERENT NOW.

"NO ONE TALKS ABOUT IT.

"THIS... THING... ERUPTS OUT OF THE GROUND... AND IT CHANGES THE COLOR OF THE DAMN SKY.

"AND PEOPLE JUST... ACCEPT IT.

"LIKE IT'S NATURAL OR SOMETHING.

"THAT JUST DOESN'T SEEM RIGHT..."

...DOES IT?
FRANKIE! FRANKIE!
LOOK WHAT I FOUND!
AN *ARTIFACT!*

HEY... *UH...* ***ISAAC,*** RIGHT?
LET'S SEE WHAT YOU HAVE THERE.
I THINK IT'S ANOTHER ***GOD.***

TELL YOU WHAT...
...YOU GO OUTSIDE AND TRY TO FIND SOME MORE, ALL RIGHT?
I NEED TO FINISH TALKING TO ***DR. KINDER.***
BUT I'LL BE OUT SOON AND WE CAN FIGURE OUT WHAT YOU'VE FOUND.

HE LIKES YOU.
HE LATCHED ONTO YOU PRETTY QUICKLY.
HE HASN'T DONE THAT WITH ANYONE SINCE HIS PARENTS LEFT.

LEFT?

PEOPLE JOIN US-- LIKE YOU.
THEY WANT ANSWERS-- LIKE YOU.
SOMETIMES, THEY DON'T FIND WHAT THEY'RE LOOKING FOR.

AND THEY JUST LEAVE THEIR KIDS BEHIND?

LIKE YOU SAID...
...EVERYTHING'S DIFFERENT NOW.

YOU'RE DIFFERENT NOW, ALEX.
YOU WERE THE PROFESSOR WHO MADE ME WANT TO PURSUE SCIENCE.
NOW, THOUGH, YOU'RE A MAN OF--
FAITH.
WHEN A GOD-- *AN ACTUAL GOD*-- APPEARS... IT CAN SHAKE YOUR BELIEF SYSTEM.

IT'S A *TOY*.
PROBABLY LEFT OVER...
...FROM BEFORE THIS WAS A *COMMUNE*.

DON'T WORRY, FRANKIE.
HENRY WILL HELP YOU FIND YOUR FAITH, TOO.
HENRY--

DID SOMEONE SAY MY NAME?

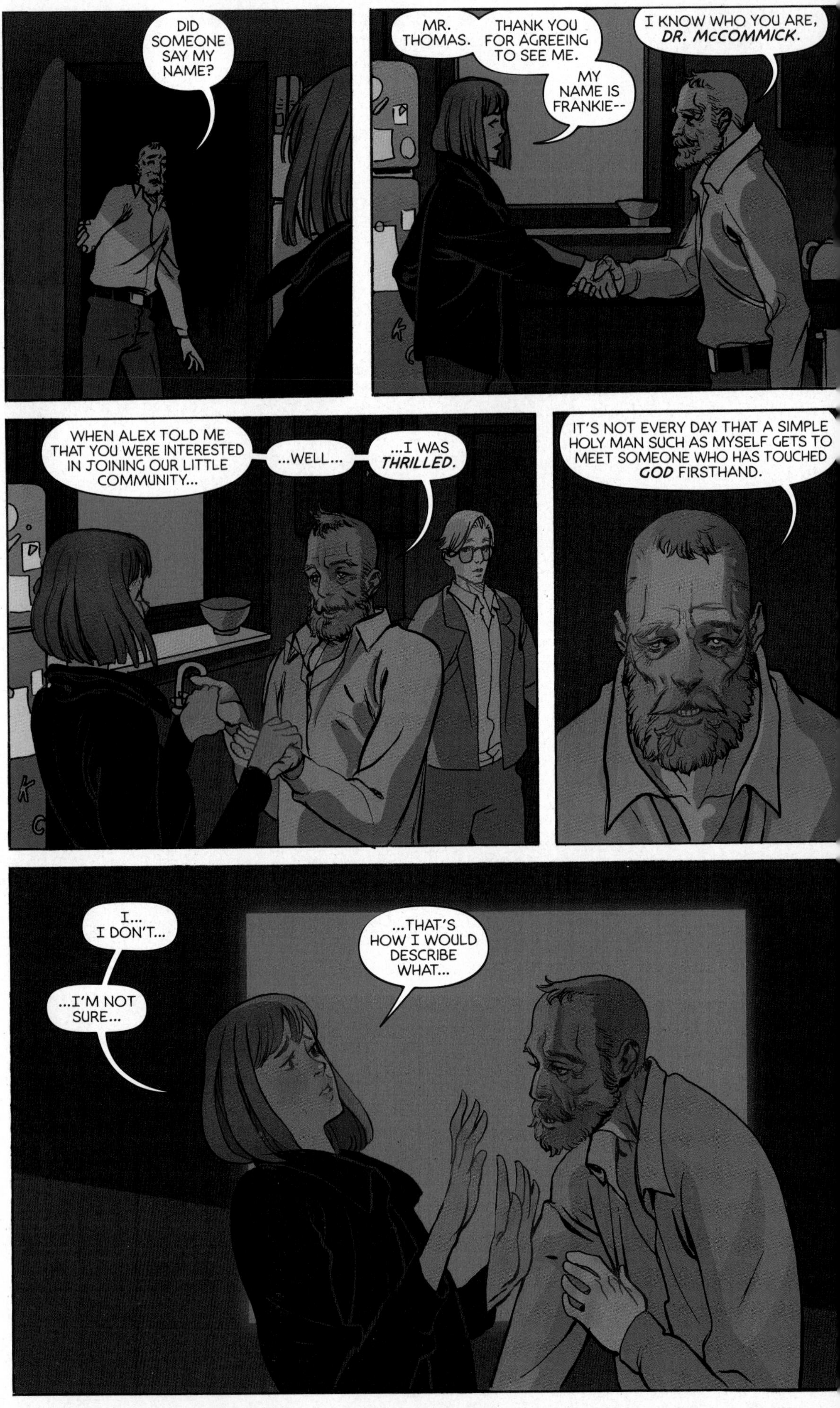

MR. THOMAS.
THANK YOU FOR AGREEING TO SEE ME.
MY NAME IS FRANKIE--
I KNOW WHO YOU ARE, ***DR. McCOMMICK***.

WHEN ALEX TOLD ME THAT YOU WERE INTERESTED IN JOINING OUR LITTLE COMMUNITY...
...WELL...
...I WAS ***THRILLED***.

IT'S NOT EVERY DAY THAT A SIMPLE HOLY MAN SUCH AS MYSELF GETS TO MEET SOMEONE WHO HAS TOUCHED ***GOD*** FIRSTHAND.

I... I DON'T...
...I'M NOT SURE...
...THAT'S HOW I WOULD DESCRIBE WHAT...

HUSH, CHILD. HUSH.
DON'T TRY TO PUT THE *UNSPEAKABLE* INTO WORDS.
SOME THINGS ARE NOT MEANT TO BE UNDERSTOOD.
WE MUST SIMPLY... ACCEPT THEM.

LIKE THE SKY.

THE SKY?
DID YOU--
WERE YOU LISTENING?

IT'S ALL RIGHT.
WHAT YOU'VE BEEN THROUGH...
...WELL...
...IT'S NO WONDER YOU'RE *HAUNTED.*

AFTER ALL, IT'S A ONCE IN A LIFETIME EXPERIENCE, IS IT NOT?

I MEAN... HOW MANY GODS DO YOU THINK ARE JUST SLEEPING UNDERGROUND?

THEY WANT TO KNOW WHY THESE THINGS ARE MISBEHAVIN'.

FIGHTIN' INSTEAD OF BEIN' DOCILE.

LIKE THERE'S JUST GOT TO BE SOME DAMN REASON.

FOR EVERYTHING.

RIDLEY FUCKING SCOTT.

ARE THESE SKINS?
JUST DISCARDED HUSKS.
LIKE THEY'RE MOLTIN'.

WHAT THE HELL?
PLIP

YOU KNOW WHAT IT IS.
WHAT DO YOU THINK LEFT THESE SKINS BEHIND?
WHAT DO YOU THINK THEY TURNED INTO?

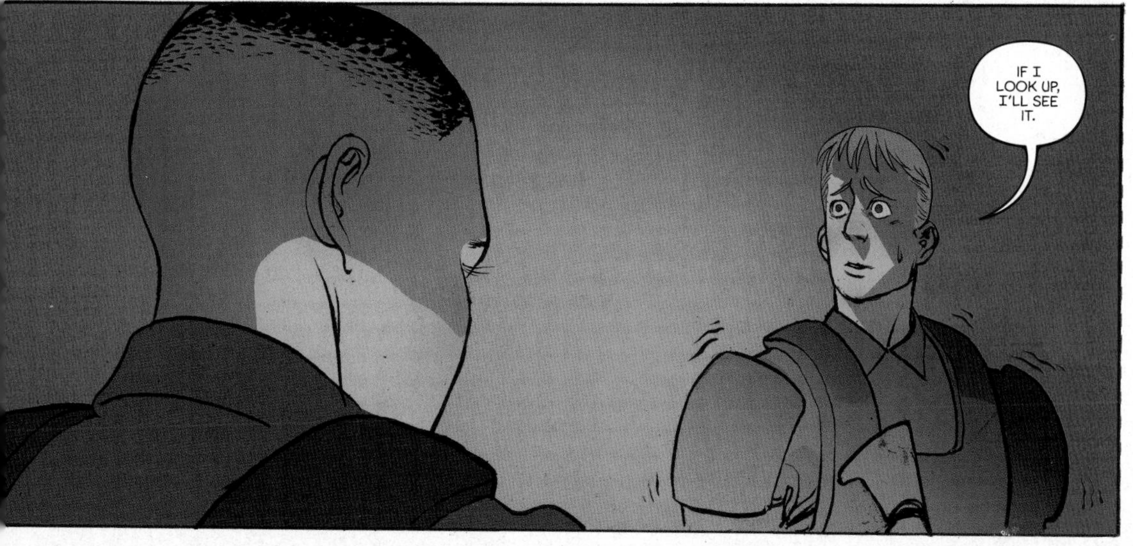
IF I LOOK UP, I'LL SEE IT.

SUIT
YOURSELF.

THEN.
"SPEAK TO ME, LORD."

YOU BROUGHT HER TO ME.
THIS MUST BE A SIGN.
I HAVE BEEN ***FAITHFUL.***

BUT SHE DOUBTS.
SHE HAS ***SEEN*** YOUR ***REBIRTH.***
SHE HAS SEEN ***RECLAMATION.***

THE FLESH OF THE WEAK BECOMING THE FLESH OF THE STRONG.
THE FLESH OF MANY BECOMING THE FLESH OF ONE.
THE MIND OF ONE BECOMING THE MIND OF MANY.

SHE IS ***BLESSED.***
YET SHE ***DOUBTS.***
AND IN HER DOUBT, LORD, YOU HAVE SHOWN ME THE WAY.

FOR I WILL SHOW HER WHAT FAITH CAN DO.
I WILL SHOW HER WHAT WE CAN BRING INTO THE WORLD.
AND I, TOO, WILL BE BLESSED.

FHTAGN.

Ch 07

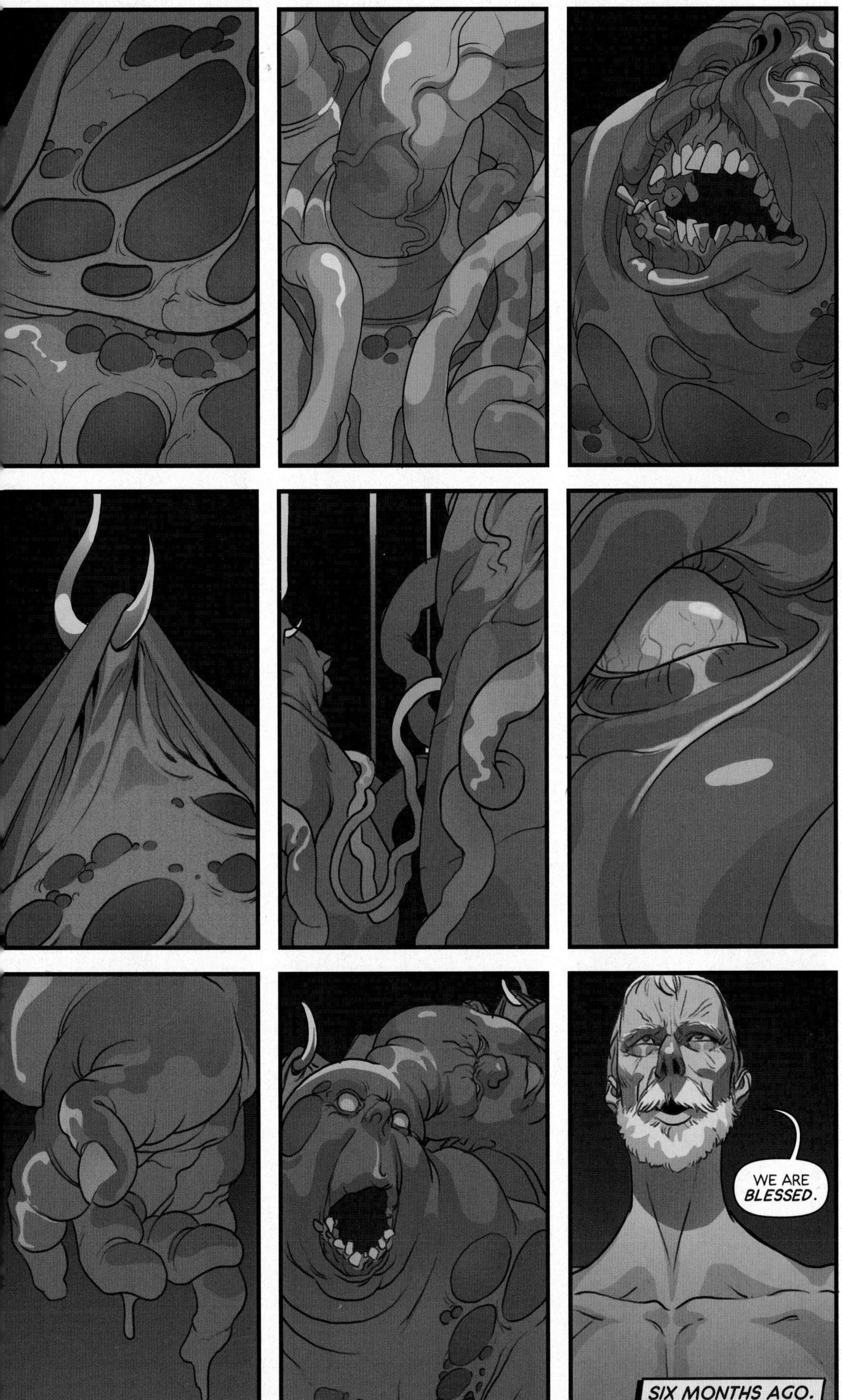
WE ARE BLESSED.
SIX MONTHS AGO.

WE SHOULD ALL BE THANKFUL.
OUR FRIENDS HAVE VOLUNTEERED.
THEY HAVE OFFERED THEMSELVES UP...
...FOR *TRANSFIGURATION!*
BLESSED.
AND SOON, LIKE OUR SWOLLEN BRETHREN.
WE WILL BE READY TO *DESCEND*.
WE WILL *ALL* BE MADE READY.

NOW.
"I'VE BEEN BABYSITTING THIS FUCKER FOR MONTHS."
MONTHS.
AND WE STILL DON'T KNOW HOW TO KILL IT.
OUR WEAPONS ARE USELESS.
WE CAN'T GET PLANES OR TANKS CLOSE TO IT BEFORE IT JUST SHUTS THEM DOWN.
I'VE GOT FIELD REPORTS AND ENVIRONMENTAL ANALYSIS AND SCIENTIFIC SPECULATION.
GIGS OF DATA.
AND YOU KNOW WHAT IT TELLS ME?
KRAK
FUCK-ALL, THAT'S WHAT!
YOU WILL NOT BE ABLE TO KILL IT.
IT IS A HIGHER BEING.
IT CANNOT BE KILLED.

NOT LIKE US.
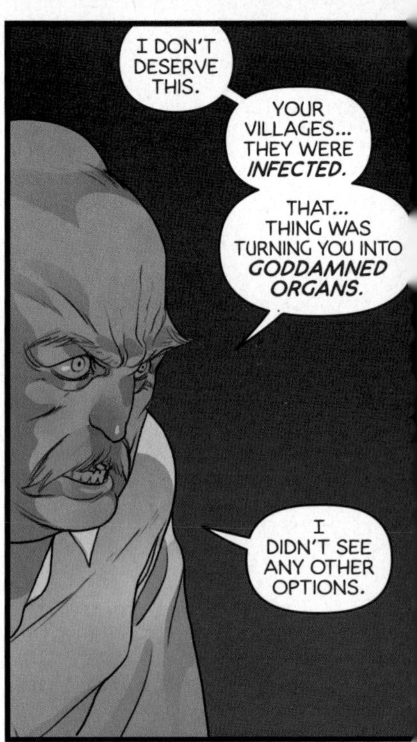
I DON'T DESERVE THIS.
YOUR VILLAGES... THEY WERE *INFECTED.*
THAT... THING WAS TURNING YOU INTO ***GODDAMNED ORGANS.***
I DIDN'T SEE ANY OTHER OPTIONS.

AND YET *IT* CONTINUES TO *GROW.*
IT BECOMES WHAT IT ONCE WAS.
IT GRASPS FOR THE *INFINITE.*

YOU MUST SEEK SOMETHING MORE.
YOU MUST SEEK *UNDERSTANDING.*
SEEK WHAT YOU HAVE *DENIED* US.

IT AIN'T RIGHT.
I SHOULDN'T BE *PUNISHED* LIKE THIS.
I CAN'T BE THE ONLY ONE...

"...HAUNTED BY THE THINGS I'VE DONE."

THEN.

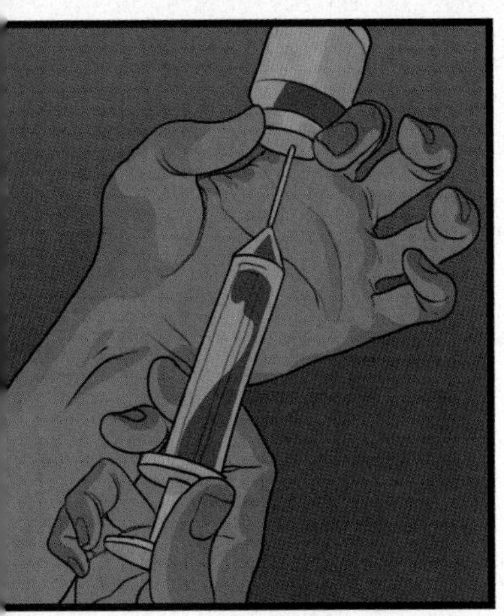

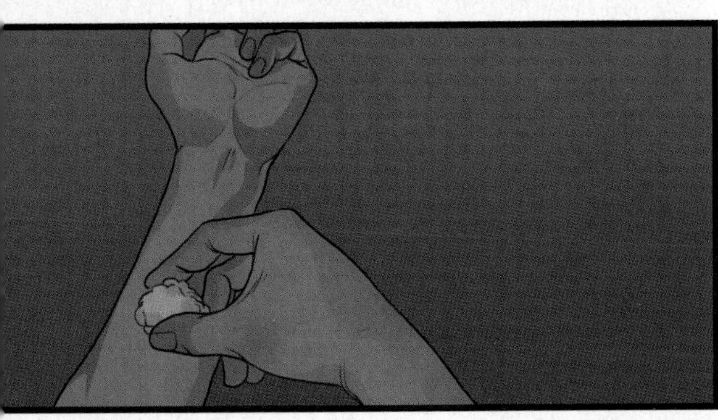

IT MIGHT NOT BE THE WAY YOU WANT TO GO.

IT'S ALL I HAVE, BOSS.

FOR SIX MONTHS YOU'VE BEEN CLUE-HUNTING WITH EVERY JIM JONES LOSER YOU CAN FIND.
NOW YOU'RE GOING TO CANCEL YOUR SVENGALI-OF-THE-MONTH MEMBERSHIP RIGHT BEFORE THE GOOD STUFF?

THE WORK IS...
...EMPTY.

THAT'S WHAT I WAS THINKING RIGHT BEFORE YOU STABBED ME IN MY FUCKING NECK.
YOU HAVE A BIG PUZZLE TO SOLVE, FRANKIE. IT'S WHAT YOU OWE ME.
YOU DON'T QUIT UNTIL THE WORK IS DONE.
AFTER THAT...

...GO AHEAD AND BURN YOUR VEINS TO ASH.

NOW.
F-FALL BACK.
EVERYBODY... GET TO COVER.
FALL BACK.

THESE SLUGS... ALWAYS DOCILE.

"'TIL NOW."
KRASH

"WHAT'S CHANGING?"
N-NAILS... THERE AIN'T NO GETTING CLEAR.

"WHY ARE THEY TURNING MEAN?"
HRRRR--

"THEY... WANT SOMETHING."
I'VE GOT THIS FUCKER!

"THEY'LL KILL FOR IT."
NAILS!

ARE YOU CLEAR?

I'M ABOUT TO BE.

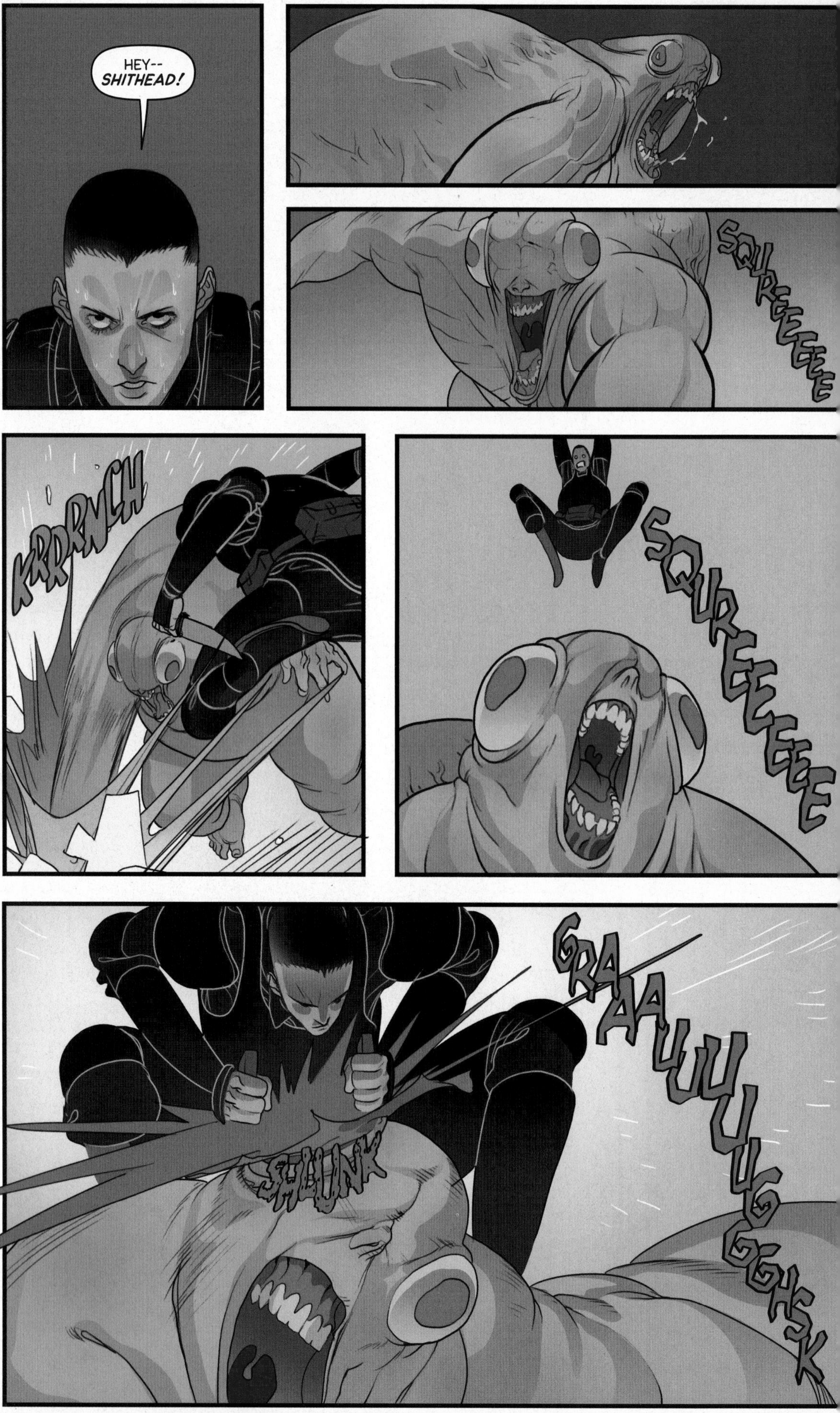

GRAAAUUUGGHSK

SHUNK

NOW, I'M ALL CLEAR.

THEY'RE JUST HOLDING THE LINE... KEEPING US BUSY.
GOD KNOWS HOW MANY OF THEIR BIG BROTHERS ARE GETTING LOOSE WHILE THEY KEEP US KETTLED HERE.

CAN'T WASTE TIME WITH THESE GUYS.

BUT CHECK IT.
UP THERE.
THAT THING.

WE CAN'T LET MOM ESCAPE THE BLACKOUT ZONE.

THEN.

FRANKIE!
COME JOIN US!

COME ON!
OVER HERE!
YOU CAN SIT BY ME!

ISAAC-- DON'T MAKE SUCH A FUSS.
IT'S ALL RIGHT.
HE'S NOT BOTHERING ME.

WELL, MAYBE *YOU* CAN CONVINCE HIM NOT TO PLAY NEAR THE CAVES, *HM?*
WE'VE CAUGHT HIM TRYING TO HEAD THAT WAY THREE TIMES NOW.
MY PARENTS ARE THERE, THAT'S WHY.

MAYBE THEY ARE.
BUT YOU'RE NOT OLD ENOUGH.
YOU'RE NOT READY.

CHILDREN!

I ONLY WANTED TO SEE THEM AGAIN...
...BEFORE THEY AREN'T MY PARENTS ANYMORE.

"BUT SHE'S KEEPING US DISTRACTED."

THOOM

THOOM

THOOM

KLIK

LET'S SLOW HER DOWN.

KRAKAKOOM

SGLLLKK

YEEEAAAAARGH!
I ASKED FOR THAT DAMN RPG!
BRAKKA
BRAKKA

HUP!

WHOOOM

W-WE DID IT?
RIGHT?
I MEAN... IT'S DEAD, RIGHT?

ONE OF THEM IS DEAD.
JUST ONE.
IT BOUGHT ALL THE OTHERS TIME TO GET OUT OF HERE.

THEY'RE SPREADING OUT.
THEY'RE LEAVING THE BLACKOUT ZONE.
AND I DON'T KNOW IF WE CAN STOP THEM.

"TAKE A GOOD LONG LOOK AT THAT BEAST."

I WAS RIGHT THERE WHEN THAT THING HATCHED.
IT WAS LIKE A GODDAMNED NEST OF EELS MIXED WITH SOMETHING STRAIGHT OUTTA A TOKYO MONSTER MOVIE.
HEH HA HEH!
AND NOW IT'S BALLED ITSELF UP LIKE A ROLY-POLY BUG.

YOU KNOW WHAT THAT SAYS TO ME?
SAYS IT'S SCARED.
SAYS IT THINKS WE CAN HURT IT.

IT WAS CHANGING PEOPLE IN THE BLACKOUT ZONE.
STILL TRYING TO HEAL ITSELF.
BUT NOW IT'S SENDING THESE POOR BASTARD MUTANTS OUT... LIKE ANTENNAE.
LIKE FEELERS.

IT'S LOOKING FOR SOMETHING.
AND I'M GONNA MAKE SURE IT NEVER FINDS IT.
I'M DISPATCHING TEAMS TO HUNT DOWN THOSE MUTANTS AND KILL THEM BEFORE THEY GET WHEREVER THE HELL THEY'RE GOING.

YOU LUCKY BASTARDS GET TO RIDE WITH ME.

WE BUG OUT AT DAWN.
SO GET SOME DAMN REST.
SAY YOUR PRAYERS, YOU MISERABLE SHITS.

HAH HEH HAH.

FUCK IT.

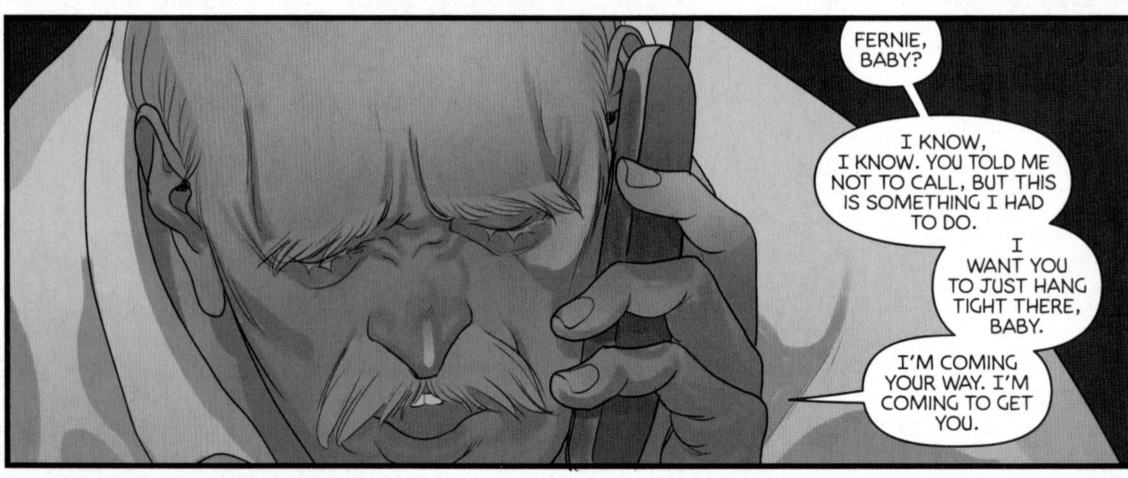
FERNIE, BABY?
I KNOW, I KNOW. YOU TOLD ME NOT TO CALL, BUT THIS IS SOMETHING I HAD TO DO.
I WANT YOU TO JUST HANG TIGHT THERE, BABY.
I'M COMING YOUR WAY. I'M COMING TO GET YOU.

THEN.

HM?

DAMMIT!

ISAAC?

ISAAC!
WAIT!
WHERE ARE YOU GOING?

HEY, FRANKIE.
YOU SHOULDN'T BE OUT HERE WITHOUT SHOES. YOU'LL GET SPLINTERS.
I'M JUST GOING DOWN TO THE CAVES.
MY PARENTS ARE DOWN THERE AND I WANT TO SEE THEM.

WOULD YOU LIKE TO COME WITH ME?

I...
...
YES.
YES, I THINK I WOULD.

ELSEWHERE.

OUR
KING
IS PATIENT.

SIX MONTHS AGO.
THIS WAY, FRANKIE!

ISAAC-- WAIT.
HOW CAN YOU EVEN BE SURE WHERE YOU'RE GOING?

MY PARENTS ARE DOWN HERE!
THEY'RE CALLING TO ME!
HOW CAN IT BE WRONG FOR ME TO BE HERE IF MY MOM AND DAD ARE CALLING ME?

I CAN'T WAIT FOR YOU TO MEET THEM!

SOMETHING'S WRONG.
THERE'S A SMELL.
IT'S...

THIS IS ALL TOO FAMILIAR.

DRRK-
TREEE-
DRK

DRRRRRK-
TR-DRRRK
WHAT ARE *YOU* DOING HERE?

COME ON!
THEY WON'T KNOW ME IF WE WAIT TOO LONG!
I WON'T KNOW THEM!

NOW.
THAT'S A GOOD GODDAMN LOT OF BLIPS!
LIKE PIMPLES ON A SCHOOLBOY.
EACH OF THOSE DOTS IS A VERIFIED SIGHTING.
THOSE FUCKERS WE FAILED TO KEEP IN THE BLACKOUT ZONE ARE MOVING FAST.
LUCKY FOR US THEY DIDN'T SPREAD OUT TOO MUCH.
MAYBE THEY KNOW EXACTLY WHERE THEY'RE HEADED.
HEH HA HA.
NAH, I'M JOSHIN'.
NAILS, WITH THE LIEUTENANT IN SICK BAY, YOU'RE IN CHARGE.
I HALF BELIEVE YOU WON'T FUCK IT ALL UP.
THANK YOU, SIR.

WE HAVE UNITS SETTING UP A NETWORK OF STOPGAP BARRIERS NORTHEAST OF HERE.
BASED ON THE EASE OF TERRAIN, WATERWAYS, ETC., OUR BOYS THINK THEY'VE FIGURED OUT THE MOST LIKELY DIRECTIONS THE MONSTERS WILL RUN.
THOSE THINGS ARE FAST, NAILS. THEY'RE STRONG.
AND THEY'RE *SMART.*
THEY OUTSMARTED US TO ESCAPE FROM THE BLACKOUT ZONE.
THEY'RE NOT GOING TO OUTSMART US AGAIN.
WE'RE HEADED FOR THE BARRIER OUTSIDE NASHVILLE, TENNESSEE, ON GOD'S HIGHWAY, #40.
YOU GONNA BE READY TO HANDLE WHATEVER IT IS WE HAVE TO HANDLE, NAILS?
YOU'RE GODDAMN RIGHT, SIR.
DISMISSED.

I KNOW THAT YOU KNOW I'VE SPENT A LOT OF TIME ON HIGHWAY 40, BRADLEY.
YES, SIR.
THEN IT WON'T SHOCK YOU...
...WE'RE GONNA MAKE A STOP ALONG THE WAY.

YOU'RE GODDAMNED RIGHT.

YOU SAY SOMETHING, NAILS?
I THOUGHT YOU SAID SOMETHING.
HM?

I GUESS I WAS JUST THINKING.
ABOUT HOW MUCH EVERYTHING HAS *CHANGED.*
ABOUT HOW *DIFFERENT* THE WORLD IS NOW.

WE WALKED INTO THOSE CAVES IN MEXICO.
WE LEFT OUR WORLD BEHIND.
AND WE NEVER SAW IT AGAIN.

MAKES ME THINK.
EVERY DECISION YOU MAKE...
...NO MATTER HOW SMALL...

"...PUTS A *NAIL* IN THE COFFIN OF THE WORLD THAT EXISTED BEFORE."

THEN.
ISAAC?
WHERE'D YOU GO?
WAIT FOR ME.
COME ON, ISAAC.
DON'T RUN OFF ON ME.
YOU'VE GOT THE LANTERN.

CLATTER
CLAK

WOULD YOU MIND PICKING THOSE UP FOR ME, FRANKIE?

I THINK IT WAS A ***GOOD ROLL.***

THIS...
WHAT IS IT, BOSS?
SOME SORT OF GAME?

LYDIA AND I USED TO PLAY.
IT WAS A GAME OF CONFLICT.
ELDER GODS, TRYING TO TAKE OVER THE WORLD.

BUT YOU WOULDN'T KNOW THAT, WOULD YOU?
I NEVER ***TOLD*** YOU ABOUT THE GAME.
SO MAYBE YOU SHOULD STOP THINKING SO ***SMUGLY*** ABOUT ME.
I'M ***NOT*** JUST SOME FIGMENT OF YOUR IMAGINATION.

NOW.
THIS IS IT.
I'LL BE TEN MINUTES.
NOK NOK
2022

FERNIE.
JEFF...
...WHAT ARE YOU ON ABOUT?
MIND IF I COME IN?

NOW.
IT SAYS "FIRM, SET, CERTAIN."
IT'S TEN LETTERS.
RESTRICTED AREA DO NOT ENTER
PHOTOGRAPHY OF THIS AREA IS PROHIBITED 18 USC 795
I DON'T KNOW MAN.
I'M NO GOOD AT THOSE PUZZLES.
THAT THING DOESN'T FREAK YOU THE FUCK OUT?
DOESN'T BOTHER ME.
IT DOES ME, MAN. I'VE SEEN IT A HUNDRED TIMES, BUT EVERY TIME I LOOK AT IT, I FEEL LIKE I'M LOOKING AT SOMETHING *SINISTER.*
SOMETHIN'...
...I DON'T KNOW...

SSSHHHSZZZSSS
...INEVITABLE.

SZZZZZSTTTZZZT

S-S-ZZZTSZSHHHZZZZZ

THEN.
THIS MIGHT STILL BE DELUSION.
AT LEAST, YOU MIGHT BE.
MY MIND COULD BE COOKING UP ALL SORTS OF NONSENSE ABOUT YOU.

MAYBE.
MAYBE WE'RE NOT HERE AT ALL.
MAYBE YOU DIDN'T CUT MY THROAT OUT.

CLATTER
CLATTER

NO SUCH LUCK.

WHAT IS THIS PLACE, BOSS?
WHAT WAS HANGING FROM THESE CHAINS?
IT LOOKS LIKE... A MEAT PACKING PLANT THAT TOLD THE HEALTH INSPECTOR TO FUCK OFF.

WOULDN'T IT BE SOMETHING?
IF WE WERE ALL JUST DREAMING THE *SAME* DREAM?
ALL OF US, WAITING TO *WAKE UP?*

WAKING UP... *THAT'S* THE MUTATION.

YOU FORGOT THIS.
AND YOU'LL NEED IT.
YOU'LL NEED IT BEFORE YOU'RE DONE.

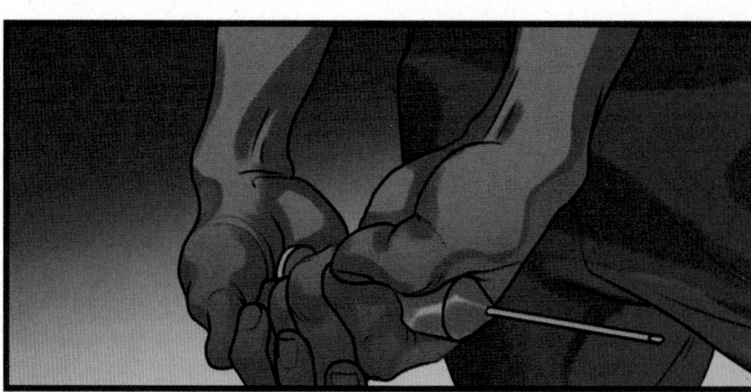

WELL... HELLO.

THIS IS AN UNEXPECTED SURPRISE.
WELCOME, DR. McCOMMICK.
IF I HAD KNOWN YOU WOULD BE JOINING US, I WOULD HAVE ARRANGED A GUIDED TOUR.
MR. THOMAS.
PLEASE.
CALL ME HENRY.
WHILE YOU STILL CAN.
YOU'RE CURIOUS ABOUT THE CHAINS.
IT'S SIMPLE, REALLY.
YOU'VE SEEN SOMETHING LIKE THIS BEFORE... IN MEXICO.

MEXICO?

THE GOD YOU AWAKENED NEEDED TO HEAL ITSELF.
IT NEEDED TO *REGENERATE.*
IT NEEDED TO HARVEST--
ORGANS.

IT WAS CAUSING PEOPLE TO MUTATE.
IT ALREADY TURNED THEM INTO ORGANS.
WHAT *ELSE* DOES IT NEED?

TIME.
IT JUST NEEDS TIME.
BUT YOU MUST UNDERSTAND...

...IT IS NOT ALONE.

ELSEWHERE.

WELCOME, HENRY THOMAS...
...TO OUR *GARDEN.*

HIGHWAY 40 BLOCKADE.
NOW.
YOU EVER WATCH THOSE GIANT MONSTER MOVIES WHEN YOU WERE A KID?

SOME GIANT TURD IN A RUBBER SUIT GOES SMASHING THROUGH A CITY...
...BREATHING ATOMIC BREATH...
...SWATTING PLANES OUTTA THE SKY...

...HOSTILE PRESENCE IS GREATER THAN ANTICIPATED.
THEY DIDN'T SPREAD OUT. THEY'RE ALL HERE.
WHERE'S THAT REQUESTED BACKUP?
THE MILITARY ALWAYS RALLIES, Y'KNOW?

WE ROLL OUT THE TANKS...
...THE ROCKET LAUNCHERS...
...LIGHTNING CANNONS, IF YOU CAN BELIEVE THAT...

BUT THE MONSTER JUST SMASHES RIGHT THROUGH THEM, LIKE THEIR BEST ISN'T NOWHERE NEAR ENOUGH.
YOU EVER WATCH THOSE MOVIES?
NO, SIR. NOT REALLY.
WELL...

...THIS IS WHAT I BET THAT FEELS LIKE.
SKREEEEEEAAAAAAAAAGH!
CHAKKA CHAKKA
CHAKKA CHAKKA
WE CAN'T HOLD THEM!
REPEAT!
WE CANNOT--

HGGRRK!
SKREEAAAK!

"YOU KNOW WHAT HAPPENED TO MY LEG?"

NOBODY EVER ASKS.
I WISH PEOPLE WOULD JUST ASK.
DIDN'T FEEL LIKE IT WAS ANY OF MY BUSINESS, NAILS.

I'VE PREPARED A LOT OF ANSWERS.
JUMPED ON A *IED* TO SAVE A FRIEND.
HANG GLIDING ACCIDENT.
SHARK ATTACK WHILE SURFING IN AUSTRALIA.

THAT ONE'S MY FAVORITE.

AT LEAST IT'S MORE GLAMOROUS THAN THE TRUTH.

"HAVING A MONSTER CENTIPEDE WRAPPED TIGHT...
"...ITS NEEDLE-LEGS DIGGING INTO MUSCLE...
"...INTO BONE...
"...AND MY PARTNER--RODRIGUEZ--TURNING IT... AND MY LEG... INTO HAMBURGER."
SHARK ATTACK, *HUH?*
THAT'S ***INTENSE.***
ALWAYS WANTED TO GO TO AUSTRALIA, THOUGH.
WE'VE ALWAYS GOT THAT, RIGHT?
PEOPLE, I MEAN.
WE CAN ALWAYS SHAPE OUR OWN LITTLE FANTASY LIVES...

"...WHEN REALITY IS JUST TOO *SHITTY* TO HANDLE."

I DON'T HAVE MUCH.
BUT LET ME GET YOU SOMETHING.
SOME TEA?
COFFEE?

I CAME TO TAKE YOU AWAY FROM THIS PLACE.
I WANT TO MAKE SURE YOU'RE SAFE.

JEFF?
YOU...
...WERE WORRIED ABOUT *ME?*

OF COURSE, I WAS.
FERNIE, I KNOW I'VE DONE WRONG.
I KNOW I LET THE JOB GET IN THE WAY OF OUR LIFE TOGETHER.
BUT I WANT TO MAKE IT RIGHT.

IT TOOK THE WORLD FALLING DOWN AROUND OUR EARS...
...IT TOOK ME DOING THOSE *AWFUL* THINGS...
...TO REALIZE HOW *LOST* I WAS.

AWFUL THINGS?

I NEEDED TO SAVE THE WORLD.

I WAS OUT OF OPTIONS.

THE INFECTION WAS SPREADING, YOU SEE.

WHAT DID YOU DO?

I DESTROYED VILLAGES.

BLASTED THEM ALL TO HELL.

KILLED HUNDREDS OF PEOPLE.

HUNDREDS...

AND I THOUGHT...

...MAYBE...

...IF I COULD SAVE YOU...

...IT MIGHT ALL BE WORTH IT.

SIR--THE BARRICADE.
IT'S BEEN *OVERRUN.*
THOSE MONSTERS LEFT A TRAIL. OUR UNITS ARE IN PURSUIT.

FOLLOW 'EM.

SEE?
WE ALL CREATE OUR OWN LITTLE REALITIES.
AND SOMETIMES...

...EVEN OUR FANTASIES *PUNISH* US.

SIX MONTHS AGO.
HOW MANY GODS DO YOU THINK ARE SLEEPING UNDERGROUND?
MORE THAN ONE, I CAN ASSURE YOU.
I WANT TO SHOW YOU WHAT I HAVE LEARNED.

THE GODS DO NOT BRING HORROR AND CALAMITY.
THEY BRING *HAPPINESS.*
THEY BRING *PEACE.*
BUT YOU MUST *ACCEPT IT,* DR. McCOMMICK.

THE PEOPLE YOU HAD CHAINED.
DID *THEY* ACCEPT IT?

OH, YES.
COME WITH ME.
LET ME SHOW YOU.

SOME RESISTED.
THEY REQUIRED... ***INDOCTRINATION.***
BUT THEY ARE ALL SO MUCH HAPPIER NOW.
ISAAC!
ARE YOU--
I'M JUST FINE, FRANKIE.
SEE?
I FOUND THEM!
I FOUND MY MOM AND DAD!

WHAT ARE YOU DOING HERE?
THIS IS... AN *ABOMINATION!*
WHAT ARE YOU DOING TO THESE PEOPLE?
IT IS NECESSARY.
OUR FLESH IS ONLY TEMPORARY.
ONLY RAW MATERIALS FOR THE COMING OF THE GODS.

IN MEXICO... PEOPLE MUTATED BECAUSE OF A VIRAL INFECTION.
BUT HERE...
YOU'RE *TORTURING* THESE PEOPLE.

THEY SUFFER, YES.
THEY WERE INFECTED, YES, BUT NOT BY A VIRUS.
BY A *REPRESSED COSMIC MEMORY.*
I JUST NEEDED TO REMIND THEM.

YOU... YOUR FOLLOWERS...
...WEREN'T MUTATING...
...YOU WERE DENIED...
...AND SO YOU FOUND ANOTHER WAY...

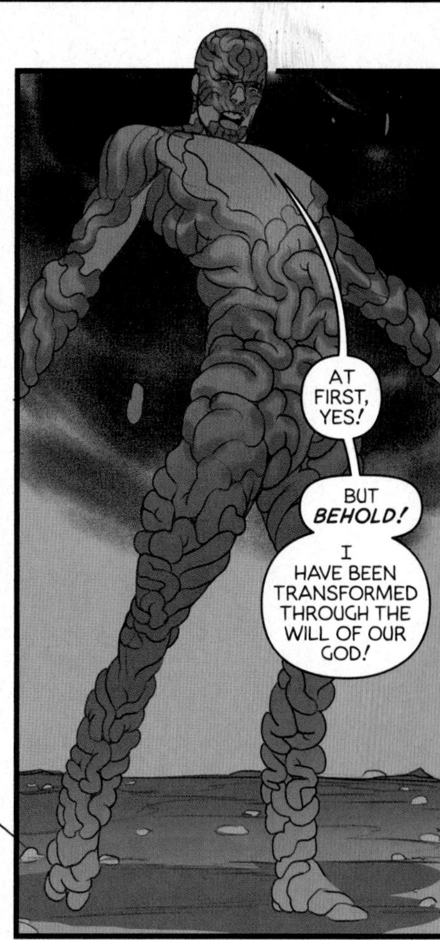
AT FIRST, YES!
BUT *BEHOLD!*
I HAVE BEEN TRANSFORMED THROUGH THE WILL OF OUR GOD!

HRRGH.
FFFF...

FFFRANKIE?
WHAT--

FRANKIE?
CAN YYOU SEEEE ME?
CAN YOU HEAARR MEEEE?
...SO MUCH EFFORT... TO COMMUNICATE THROUGH FLESSSSHHH...

IT'SSS ME FRANKIE. IT'S KING.
I NEEED YOU TO BELIEVE ME.
I NEEED YOU TO LISTEN.

YOU'RE NOT REAL.
YOU'RE A HALLUCINATION.
YOU CAN'T BE REAL.

I'M REAL.
AND I LIVE ONNN.

BUT THEY'RE NOT CRUEL.
THOSE WHO MERGE WITH THEM LIVE ON.
IT'S BEAUTIFUL HERE.
IT'S *PARADISE*.

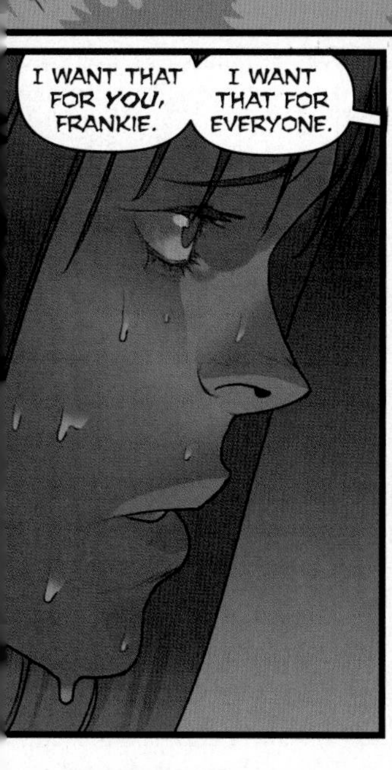

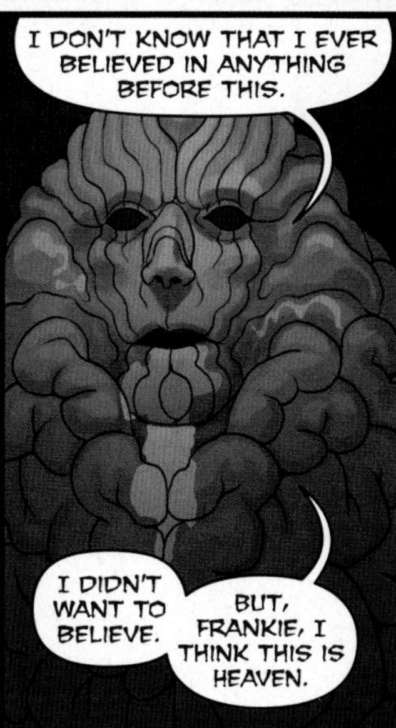

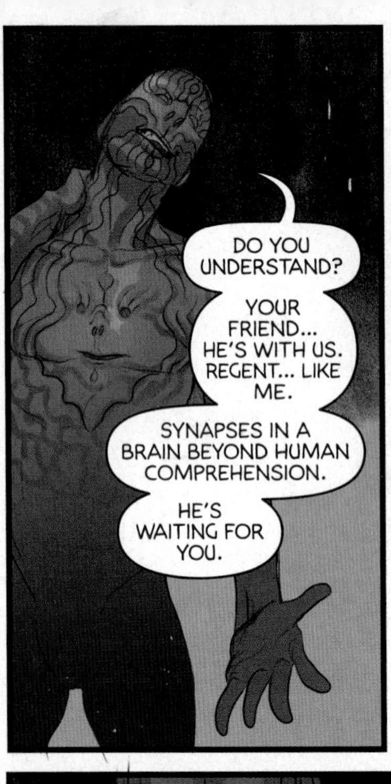
DO YOU UNDERSTAND?
YOUR FRIEND... HE'S WITH US. REGENT... LIKE ME.
SYNAPSES IN A BRAIN BEYOND HUMAN COMPREHENSION.
HE'S WAITING FOR YOU.

I'M SUPPOSED TO BELIEVE...
...THAT WE DON'T JUST DIE...
...WHEN WE BECOME ONE WITH THAT THING?

WE LIVE FOREVER.

IT'S PEACEFUL.
IT'S BEAUTIFUL.
I'VE SEEN IT.
FRANKIE!
IT'S *GOT* ME, FRANKIE!
IT WON'T LET GO!
I'M SCARED!

HOLD ON, ISAAC! I'VE GOT YOU!

YOU'D DENY THIS SQUIRT PARADISE?
THE WAY YOU DENIED IT TO ME?

BOSS?
I WANT WHAT YOU *OWE* ME, FRANKIE.
YOU HAVE A BIG PUZZLE TO SOLVE. AND YOU JUST FOUND OUT WHERE TO FIND THE ANSWERS.

KING WASN'T LYING.
AND HE USED TO CALL *ME* THE BIG BRAIN.

KING?

YOU MADE THE RIGHT CHOICE.

THE BOY DOESN'T DESERVE TO WITNESS WHAT WILL BEFALL THOSE WHO RESIST.
HE DESERVES SALVATION.

ALL THESE PEOPLE *DESERVED* A CHOICE.
AND YOU--

--YOU CAN GO TO HELL!
HHHT!
WHAT IS THIS?
WHAT DID YOU DO?
YOU... YOU... KILLED ME.
FHTAGN.
FHTAGN.

RMMMBBL
RMMMMMBBBL
KKRAK
KRAK
KRAKK
KING...
...I HOPE THAT WAS YOU...
...AND NOT JUST A FIGMENT OF MY IMAGINATION...
RMMMMMMMMMBLLL

NOW.
THE TRAIL LED HERE, SIR.
UNITS WERE ON THEIR HEELS, BUT THIS IS WHERE THE CREATURES VANISHED.
PLACE IS DESERTED, SIR.
LOOKS LIKE IT HAS BEEN FOR A WHILE.

WELL THE BEASTS ARE HERE FOR SOME REASON. THEY WENT SOMEWHERE. STAY SHARP. FOLLOW THEIR SNOT.

MAYBE THEY'RE HIDING DOWN HERE...
...IN THESE CAVES.
I DON'T LIKE IT.

ANOTHER DAMN CAVE.

DO YOU GUYS HEAR THAT?
IT SOUNDS ALMOST LIKE--
I DON'T HEAR A DAMN THING.

CLATTR
KLAK

DICE?
LOOKS LIKE THEY'RE CARVED FROM BONE OR SOMETHING.
HEY, NAILS.
FRANKIE...?
WANT TO JOIN ME FOR A GAME?

THAT'S ***NOT*** FRANKIE.

DO YOU REMEMBER ***MYSCELI ETHUSA***, NAILS?

MEXICAN BLUEWING BUTTERFLIES. THEY WERE OUR GUIDES FROM THE CAVES WHERE THE ***BEASTMOTHER*** SLEPT.

YOU AND ME, ***TOGETHER***.

THE ***ONLY*** TWO TO WALK OUT.

BEEN SEARCHING FOR ERS SINCE WE LEFT THE ES THAT DAY, NAILS.

ULD YOU) HEAR MY DINGS?

I ***WANT*** YOU TO GO TO ***HELL***.

NAILS.

LET'S HEAR WHAT SHE HAS TO SAY.

"WHEN TRIBES OF HOMININI WERE FIRST MENDING BROKEN BONES ON EARTH...
"...THE *YTHOG-RAA* HAD ALREADY MAPPED THE GENOME OF THE COSMOS."

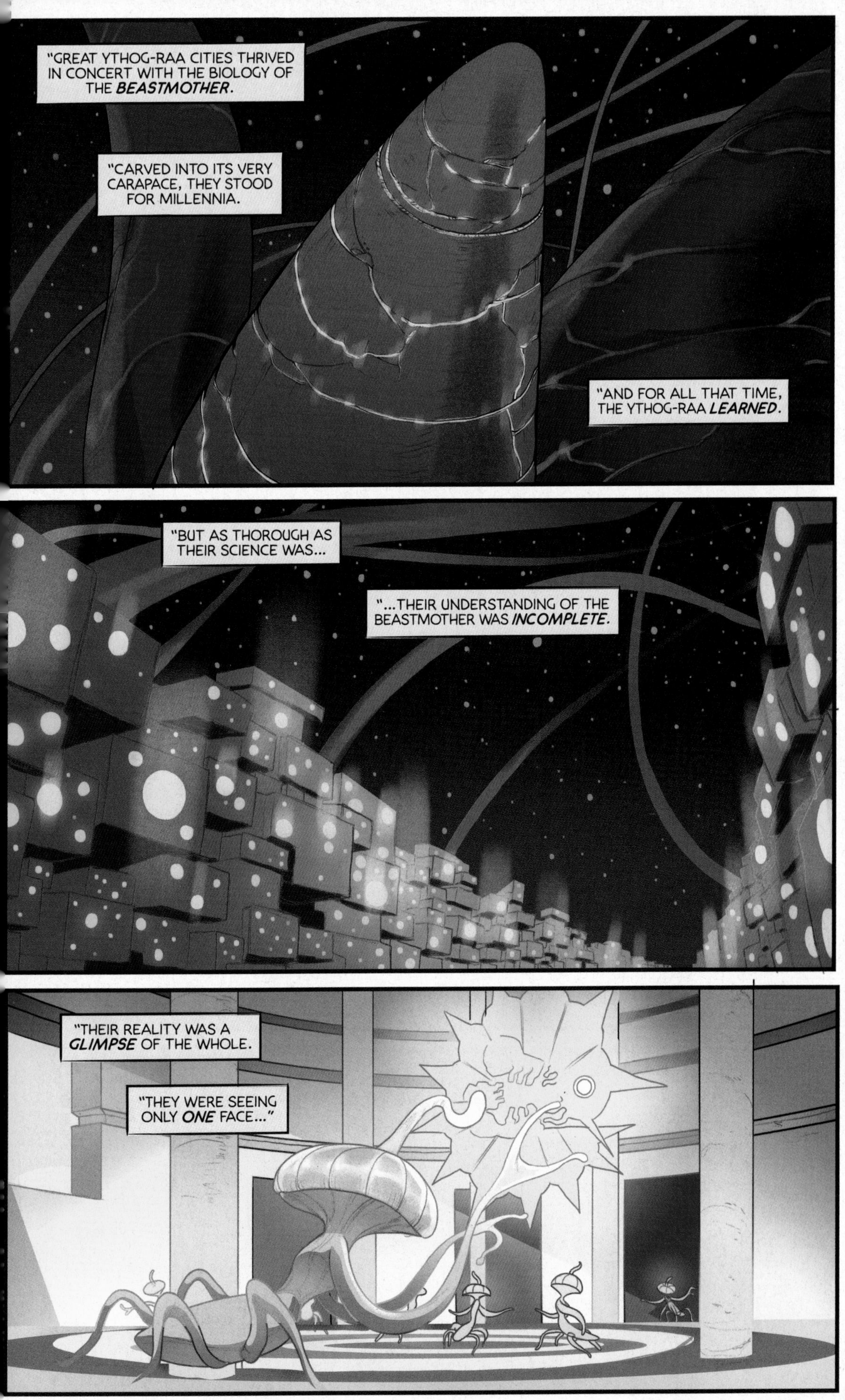
"GREAT YTHOG-RAA CITIES THRIVED IN CONCERT WITH THE BIOLOGY OF THE BEASTMOTHER.
"CARVED INTO ITS VERY CARAPACE, THEY STOOD FOR MILLENNIA.
"AND FOR ALL THAT TIME, THE YTHOG-RAA LEARNED.
"BUT AS THOROUGH AS THEIR SCIENCE WAS...
"...THEIR UNDERSTANDING OF THE BEASTMOTHER WAS INCOMPLETE.
"THEIR REALITY WAS A GLIMPSE OF THE WHOLE.
"THEY WERE SEEING ONLY ONE FACE..."

...OF A *CUBE*.
WEIRD STUFF, RIGHT?
TO THE YTHOG-RAA, WHAT THEY THOUGHT THEY *HAD* SEEMED LIKE ALL THEY EVER WANTED.
IT SEEMED... LIKE *PARADISE*.

"BUT THE TENDRILS OF THE BEASTMOTHER STRETCHED BEYOND WHAT THE YTHOG-RAA COULD SEE...
"...OR HEAR...
"...OR TASTE OR TOUCH.

"THE BEASTMOTHER HAS NO CONCEPT OF *DESIRE*.
"IF IT DID, IT MIGHT HAVE REALIZED THAT IT *WANTED* OTHERS TO SENSE ITS EXISTENCE.
"AND PEOPLE... CRAWLING AROUND ON THE SHELL OF THE PLANET... DIDN'T EVEN UNDERSTAND WHAT THEY WERE SENSING.
"WE TRIED TO VISUALIZE IT.
"BUT WE COULDN'T COMPREHEND EITHER ULTIMATE DESPAIR OR PURE BLISS.

"WE SIMPLY... HAD TO HAVE FAITH THAT WE WERE PART OF SOMETHING BIGGER THAN OURSELVES.
"TO DO OTHERWISE WAS TO WALLOW IN THE RANDOMNESS OF OUR TERRESTRIAL LIVES.

"SO... SOMEONE... JUST A LITTLE WHILE BACK... NEAR A CAVE IN MEXICO...
"...TRIED TO *SUMMON* THIS *THING* THEY'D BEEN SENSING INTO OUR REALITY."

"THEY LEARNED THE RITUAL THROUGH UNCONSCIOUS WHISPERS.
"THEY KNEW WHAT TO DO.
"BUT THE CHOICE WAS ALWAYS THEIRS."
PH'JRRG RI-LIA'PHN MGLWGH WGAH
NNAH-TRA-DI-YGAH

PH'JRRG RI-LIA'PHN MGLWGH
WGAH NNAH-TRA-DI-YGAH

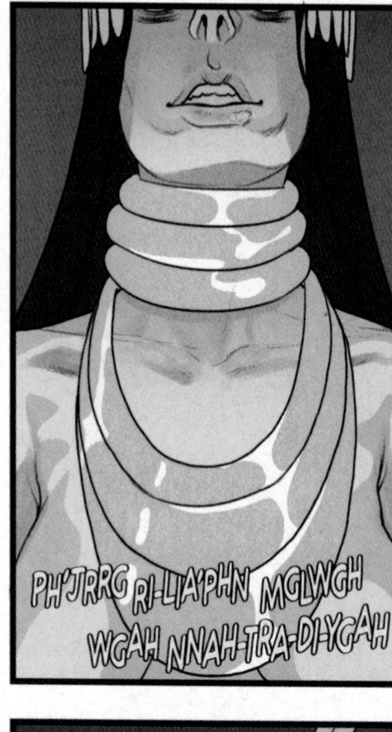
PH'JRRG RI-LIA'PHN MGLWGH
WGAH NNAH-TRA-DI-YGAH

PH'JRRG RI-LIA'PHN MGLWGH
WGAH NNAH-TRA-DI-YGAH

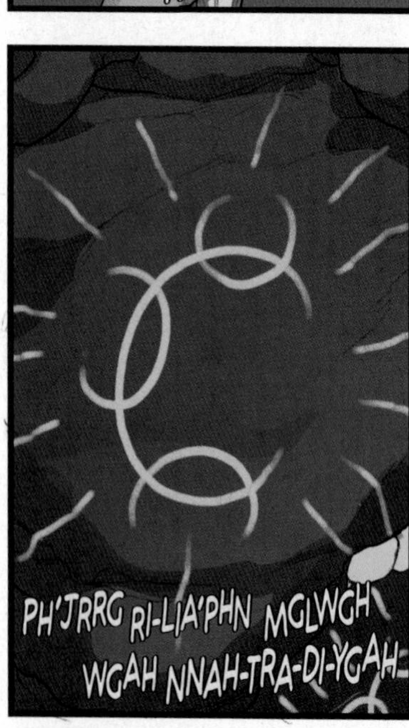
PH'JRRG RI-LIA'PHN MGLWGH
WGAH NNAH-TRA-DI-YGAH

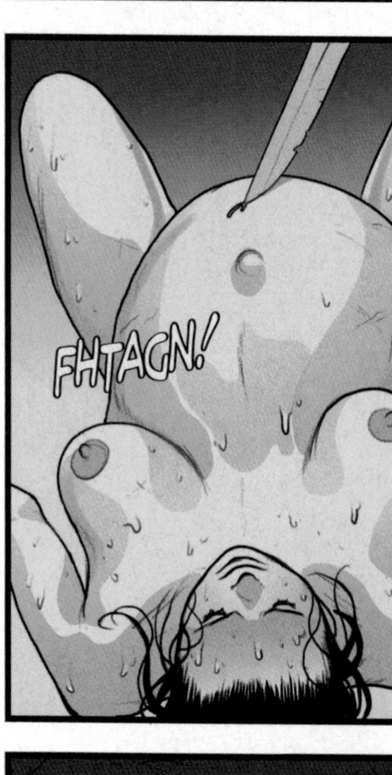
FHTAGN!

FHTAGN!

FHTAGN!!

RMMMMMBLLL

SKRAK

FHTAGN.

SO, THERE'S... *BUGS*... LIVING ON THIS THING.

YOU'RE TRYING TO TELL ME THAT REALITY IS SOME SORT OF *COSMIC ANT FARM*.
AND WE'RE ALL JUST ANTS... PUSHING GRAINS OF SAND UP AND DOWN OUR TUNNELS... HOPING THEY DON'T ROLL OVER US.
THAT'S WHAT YOU GOT OUT OF *EVERYTHING* I JUST SAID?

THAT'S... NOT TOO FAR OFF.
ONLY, YOU'RE NOT PUSHING SAND.
YOU'RE PUSHING *DICE*.

"GOD DOES NOT PLAY DICE WITH THE UNIVERSE."
YOU KNOW WHO SAID THAT?
EINSTEIN.

STOP IT!
WHOEVER YOU ARE-- JUST *STOP!*
THIS ISN'T SOME SORT OF GAME!
NO.

IT'S AN *ANT FARM*.
AND YOU CAN CHOOSE.
IS IT ONE OF THOSE NICE *TERRARIUMS?* YOU KNOW, CLEAN... WITH THE CUTE LITTLE PLASTIC FARMHOUSES ON THE SURFACE?
OR IS IT ONE OF THOSE THAT'S BEEN *NEGLECTED*... FILLED WITH THE *CARCASSES* OF THE DEAD?

WE DREW IT TO US.
BUT IT ARRIVED IN THE *PAST*, NOT THE *PRESENT*.

"TO THE BEASTMOTHER, *TIME AND SPACE* AREN'T *CONSTRAINTS.*

"THE SUMMONING RITUAL SUCCEEDED.

"BUT THE BEASTMOTHER ARRIVED IN *MANY* PLACES.
"INCLUDING OUR *DISTANT PAST.*

"NOT AS A *TYRANT*..."

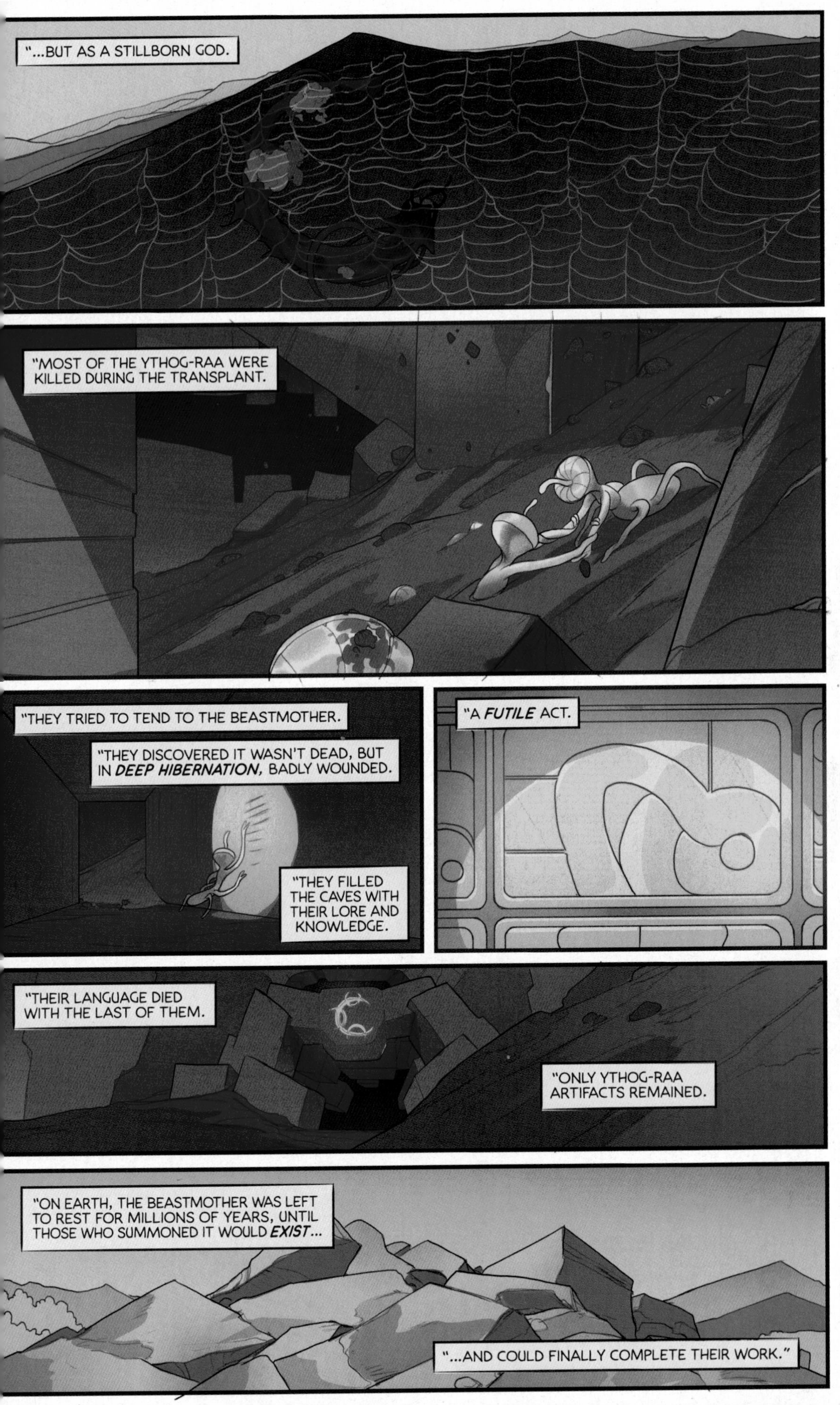
"...BUT AS A STILLBORN GOD.
"MOST OF THE YTHOG-RAA WERE KILLED DURING THE TRANSPLANT.
"THEY TRIED TO TEND TO THE BEASTMOTHER.
"THEY DISCOVERED IT WASN'T DEAD, BUT IN *DEEP HIBERNATION,* BADLY WOUNDED.
"THEY FILLED THE CAVES WITH THEIR LORE AND KNOWLEDGE.
"A *FUTILE* ACT.
"THEIR LANGUAGE DIED WITH THE LAST OF THEM.
"ONLY YTHOG-RAA ARTIFACTS REMAINED.
"ON EARTH, THE BEASTMOTHER WAS LEFT TO REST FOR MILLIONS OF YEARS, UNTIL THOSE WHO SUMMONED IT WOULD *EXIST*...
"...AND COULD FINALLY COMPLETE THEIR WORK."

"BUT IT WAS A SINGLE BEING...
EXISTING IN A MULTITUDE OF SPACES.
"ON A PLANET HUMANS HAVE NEVER EVEN DREAMED OF, THE ZADDITHIANS WORSHIPED IT.
"ACROSS THE UNIVERSE, THE KAUBA USED IT TO FUEL THEIR HERETIC BEASTS."

"EVENTUALLY HUMANITY *ATTACKED* IT.
"OR KEPT IT CAPTIVE BENEATH THE ROCK.
"BUT THE FATE OF ALL WILL BE TO WITNESS THE *REJOINING*.
"...TO *MERGE* WITH THE BEASTMOTHER AND LIVE IN *PARADISE*...
"OR TO *PERISH* IN FLAMES."

"AS THE NEXT JOINING IS ACHIEVED, AND THE NEXT.

"AND THEN THE NEXT.

"AS ALL THINGS CONVERGE.

I'VE HAD ABOUT ENOUGH OF THIS HORSESHIT.

ME TOO.

BRAAAP

SPLCT

WHERE THE HELL DID SHE GO?
I DON'T THINK SHE WAS EVER REALLY *HERE*.
"I TRIED TO HELP THEM."

I OFFERED THEM AN *OPPORTUNITY.*
PEACE AND HAPPINESS.
SO MANY FACETS ON THE DIE.
I GAVE THEM THE CHANCE TO TURN A BLIND EYE TO ONE OF THE FACETS...
...TO THE ONE THAT BRINGS PAIN AND TORMENT AND MADNESS.
I HOPE THEY'LL TAKE ME UP ON THE OFFER.
REMEMBER WHAT IT WAS LIKE TO SLEEP IN, KING?
TO JUST STAY IN BED.
EVEN WHEN YOU KNEW YOU HAD THINGS TO DO... TO ACCOMPLISH... YOU JUST LOUNGED UNDER THE COVERS?
IT FELT LIKE... ***HEAVEN.***

BUT I GUESS I CAN'T SLEEP FOREVER.
HOW'RE YOU FEELING, KING?
REFRESHED.
YOU GONNA BE OKAY WITH THIS, FRANKIE?
YEAH.
I'LL BE *FINE.*

THE BLACKOUT ZONE.
SKREEOWWW

IT'S ALL COMING DOWN!
WHAT WAS THAT SHE SAID?
RMMMMMMMBLLL
SHE SAID WE COULD KNOW PEACE!
PEACE OR DEATH!
LAST CHANCE.
YOU THE *CHURCHGOING SORT,* NAILS?
YOU SING HYMNS AND BOW YOUR HEAD AND GO TO SUNDAY SCHOOL?
YOU DRESS UP IN YOUR FRILLY WHITES AND GO TO PICNICS?
WHEN I WAS A GIRL, YEAH.
MY MOM SAID IT WAS *IMPORTANT.*
AND NOW?
MY CHURCH IS THE SAME AS YOURS.
HEH HA HEH.
ALWAYS FELT KIND OF *POINTLESS* TO ME.
IF THERE *WAS* A GOD, PEOPLE LIKE YOU AND ME WOULDN'T BE NECESSARY.
THAT'S WHAT FRANKIE-- OR WHATEVER THAT WAS--WAS OFFERING.
A WORLD WHERE WE *AREN'T* NECESSARY.

WHAT ABOUT YOU HARDCASES?
YOU FEELING NECESSARY?
YOU LOOKING FOR SOME SORT OF ***FAKE-ASS HEAVEN?***
OR DO YOU WANT TO GO TO ***HELL*** FIGHTING TOOTH AND NAIL?
GODSPEED, ASSHOLES.

"GOD-FUCKING-SPEED."

UNEARTH

THE END

BONUS FEATURE

UNSETTLED

AN UNEARTH ROMANCE BY

MARCO DEFILLO
AND KING EDDIE

Always
Carlos Ashley
<STAY AWAY FROM HER!>
<YOU HAVE NO RIGHT TO TAKE HER FROM ME!>
UNSETTLED
ART- LETTERS MARCO DEFILLO
SCRIPT- LETTERS KING EDDIE

EASY, BUDDY... DON'T GET ALL CRAZY ON US.
I DON'T THINK HE'S GONNA MOVE, GUNNY.

<PLEASE... JUST LEAVE! JUST LEAVE US ALONE!>
<SHE CAN BE SAVED, I KNOW SHE CAN BE SAVED.>

WAIT FOR MY SIGNAL... THEN TAKE HIM OUT. WE'LL HANDLE HER AFTER.
BEFORE SHE GETS AGGRESSIVE...
JUST SAY THE WORD, GUNNY.

GRRRGGLLK!!

OOF!

HUFF!
HUFF!
HUFF!

SCRACT!

HUFF...
HUFF...
HMMFF...

< I DID IT, BABY. WE ALWAYS SAID, 'YOU'RE STUCK WITH ME'... >
<... BUT YOU'LL ALWAYS BE SAFE WITH ME TOO. >

<WE'RE GOING TO FIND A WAY TO CURE YOU, MY LOVE. WE'RE GOING TO MAKE YOU NORMAL AGAIN...>

<I PROMISED I'D ALWAYS STAND BY YOU, NO MATTER WHAT. AND I ALWAYS WILL, ASH.>

CRRREEEEEEK...

< BABY??? >

"EL CAZADOR"

Art by **Kristofor Harris**
Story by **Matthew Mitchell**

CRACKLE

THIS IS RADIO TWO FOR AGENT ITZAMATUL-

COPY, RADIO TWO
WHAT'S YOUR STATUS, CANNEO?

RESCUE CASE 214 HAS BEEN DELIVERED TO SANCTUARY--
GET TO SANCTUARY SITE A2, AGENT

SIR, CASE 214 NEEDS OBSERVATION FOR--
POACHERS HAVE BEEN SPOTTED IN A2. GET THE **HELL** OVER THERE, CANNEO.

slice

YOU...
FOOL-

RANGER
USA PARKS AND WILDLIFE
..TO STOP IT-
SENT US...
ACK !!
MY FRIEND--
NO...
Kristofor

Pinup by **Scott Drummond**

Pinup by **Al Polston**

Pinup by **Gabriel Dorsey**

UNEARTH

Pinup by **Chloe Compton**

Pinup by **Tyler Beece**

With colors by **Bill Crabtree**

Pinup by **Brad Voth**

SITE 17

UNEARTh

Selected Mutations / **ISSUES 1-12**

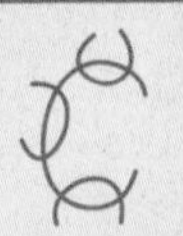

GROTESQUE HITS

Artwork by **Baldemar Rivas**

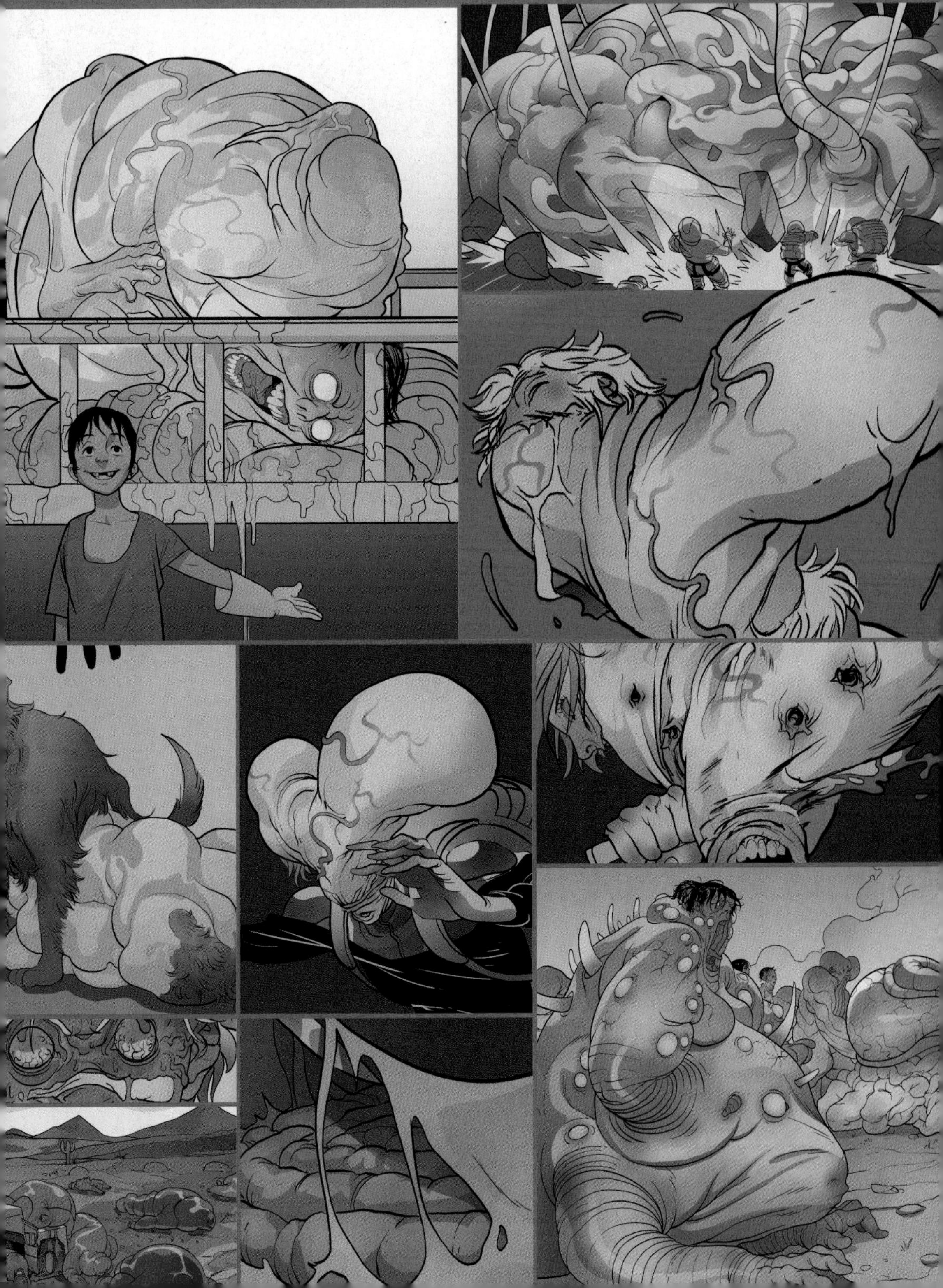

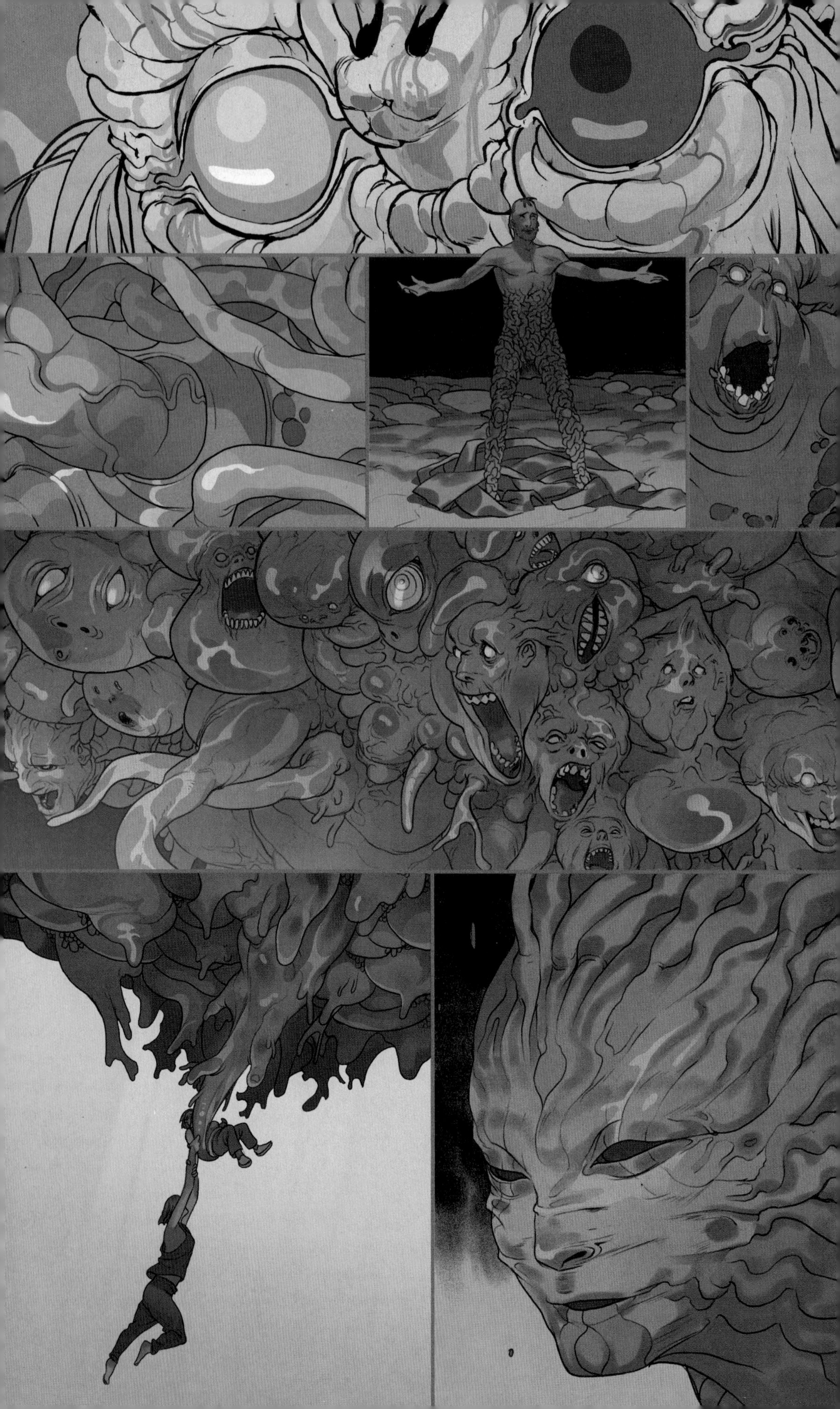

THE END

A couple of years ago, Baldemar Rivas, Cullen Bunn, and I were on a call hashing out ideas for a new comic series. Baldemar wanted to do a killer doll story, but Cullen had already done a few. You now hold in your hands the final volume of a comic that is not a killer doll story. Instead, we decided to make a weird and wet mystery about people not understanding their surroundings.

It would be impossible not to acknowledge the strange times we currently live in and how the second arc of UNEARTH, written before the Pandemic, takes place in a world where things are no longer how they've always been. I'm writing this today to say thank you all for sticking with us to the end, despite everything that's changed.

I'd also like to thank a few people who made UNEARTH happen.

Thank you to Joel Enos, our editor, who has kept us all on the path forward even though we're always running off into the weeds. There have been countless things we didn't need to worry about because we always knew you were on top of it. It's been a pleasure.

Thank you to Chris Crank who has lettered UNEARTH since we first pitched it to Image. With every project we do together you prove again and again that you're a pro, buddy.

Thank you to Ryan Brewer who designed our book from the cover dress to the easter egg back covers that connect (if you have the single issues, put them together). You've elevated every issue.

Thank you to Matthew Mitchell who managed our back matter from issue to issue (and wrote a story in this issue drawn by Kristofor Harris). You brought a new perspective to everything and a positivity that can't be faked.

Thank you Greg Smallwood who designed our logo. Now I owe you like five favors.

Thank you to everyone who has contributed pinups, backup stories, fan art, and letters. Those are the things that make single issues special and including them is one of the things I love most about making comics at Image.

Thank you to Cullen Bunn. You effortlessly solve story problems and I especially enjoy your conniving chuckle when you've thought of something terrible to do to a character. This book wouldn't have happened without you.

And finally, thank you to Baldemar Rivas. It's been a true pleasure to watch you nail your first comic gig. It's been an uncertain road, but you were always ready to get going and each new batch of pages blew me away. I'm looking forward to seeing what comes next. From the bottom of my heart, I hope it's a killer doll story.

-Kyle Strahm 1-29-2021

CULLEN BUNN is the writer of comics such as REGRESSION, COLD SPOTS, *Harrow County*, and *Manor Black*. He believes in nothing...save for the idea that he is being watched by otherworldly forces.

KYLE STRAHM was spewed from the American Heartland to write and draw dope comics. Before writing UNEARTH, Kyle created and drew the wet horror of SPREAD. He provided covers for *Bebop and Rocksteady Hit the Road*, *Green Lantern: New Guardians*, and countless titles from Image, DC, Valiant, IDW, Aftershock, Lion Forge, and Dynamite. Kyle lives and works in Kansas City, Missouri.

BALDEMAR RIVAS is an artist who has now ventured in the world of sequential storytelling. Born and raised in Visalia California, he was accepted to the Kansas City Art Institute. That is where he met Kyle Strahm and hit it off. He always carries around a sketchbook.

CRANK! Christopher Crank! (crank!) letters a bunch of books put out by Image, Dark Horse, Oni Press, Dynamite, and elsewhere. He also has a podcast with comics artist Mike Norton and members of Four Star Studio in Chicago (crankcast.com) and makes music (sonomorti.bandcamp.com). Catch him on Twitter and Instagram: @ccrank_